This Walker book belongs to:

_____

_____

_____

For Amber and Florence,
And for Emmi Cat

First published in Great Britain 2015 by Walker Books Ltd
87 Vauxhall Walk, London SE11 5HJ

This edition published 2016

2 4 6 8 10 9 7 5 3 1

© 2015 Philippa Leathers

The right of Philippa Leathers to be identified as author/illustrator of this work has
been asserted by her in accordance with the Copyright, Designs and Patents Act 1988

This book has been typeset in Aunt Mildred

Printed in China

British Library Cataloguing in Publication Data:
a catalogue record for this book is available from the British Library

ISBN 978-1-4063-6565-8

www.walker.co.uk

How to Catch a MOUSE

Philippa Leathers

WALKER BOOKS
AND SUBSIDIARIES
LONDON · BOSTON · SYDNEY · AUCKLAND

This is Clemmie.

Clemmie is a brave, fearsome mouse-catcher.

She is brilliant at stalking and chasing.

She is patient and alert.

She knows everything about
how to catch a mouse.

In fact, Clemmie is such a fearsome mouse-catcher
that she has never even seen a mouse.
All the mice are afraid of me, thinks Clemmie.

But Clemmie is always
on the look-out.

What's that?

A mouse has a long pink tail ...

but this is not a mouse.

There are no mice in *this* house!

What's that?

A mouse has two round ears ...

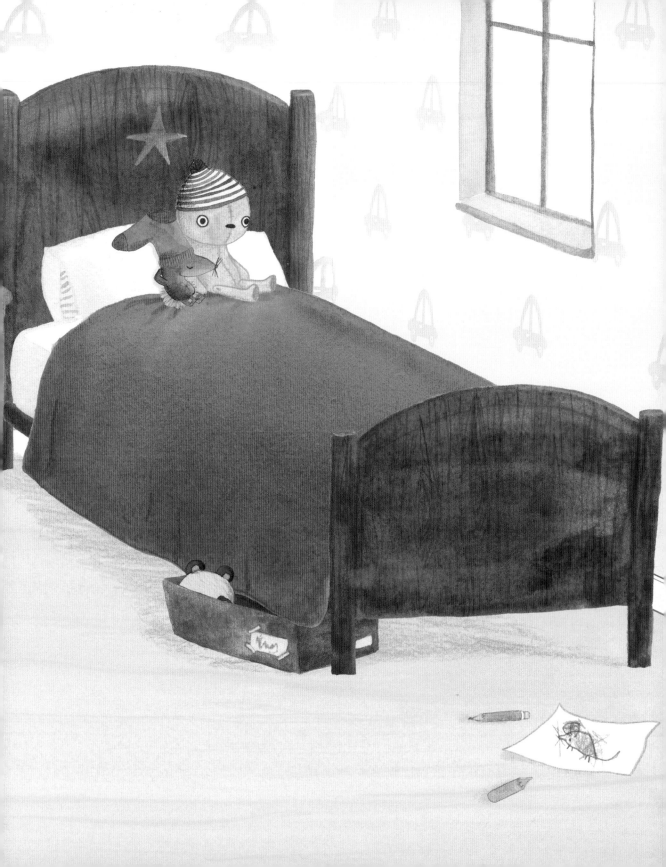

but this is not a mouse.

There are no mice in *this* house!

What's that?

A mouse has a whiskery, pointy nose ...

but this is not a mouse.

There are no mice in *this* house!

What a good mouse-scarer I am,
Clemmie thinks.
There are no mice in this house.
And she curls up for a nap.

But wait…

Crinkle!
Rustle!
Bang!

What's that?

It has a long pink tail.
It has two round ears.
It has a whiskery, pointy nose.

It's a mouse!

Clemmie has finally seen a mouse —
and it got away.

But Clemmie has learned a new trick that
might just help her catch that mouse…

Miaow!

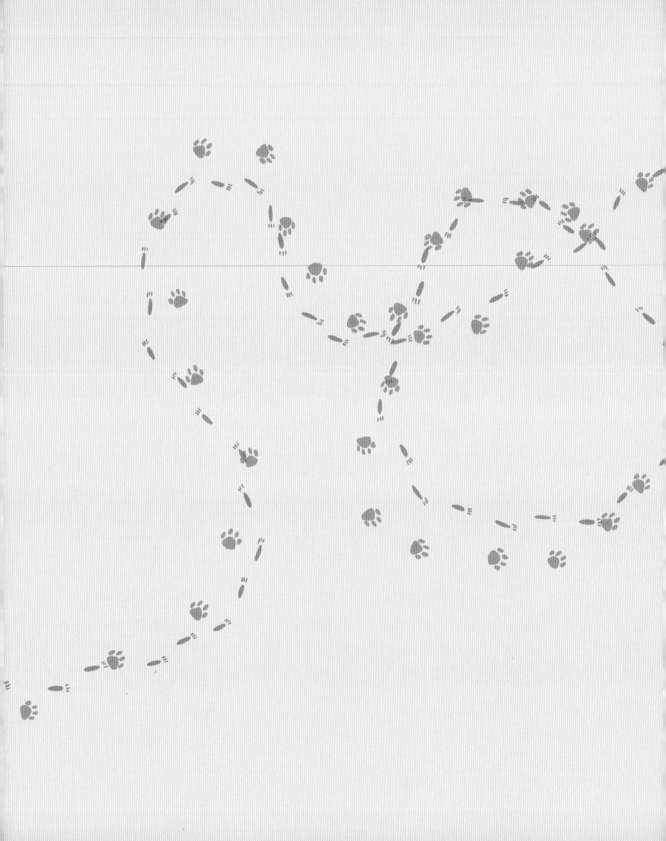

978-1-4063-5255-9

"touching" – *Guardian*

"a sweetly humorous debut" – *Wall Street Journal*

Longlisted for the Kate Greenaway Medal

Shortlisted for the Oscar's First Book Prize

A Junior Library Guild Selection

Available from all good booksellers

www.walker.co.uk